*Abandoned. The bus appeared*
*one morning from a sea of traffic—*
*right outside Stella's house,*
*where no bus should be.*
*Tired, old, and sick,*
*it had a hand-painted sign on it,*
*held down with packing tape.*

*The sign said,* **Heaven.**

*For Josephine and Alexander*

# a bus called
# heaven

## BOB GRAHAM

CANDLEWICK PRESS

The bus brought change to Stella's street.
Traffic slowed where no traffic had slowed before.
People stopped and talked together—just a little, but they talked.

Stella changed, too. She took her thumb from her mouth, where
it usually lived, and said, "Mommy, that old bus is as sad as a whale
on a beach." Then she pushed open the door and climbed on board.

Stella, the color of moonlight,
stood among the bottles, cans, and trash.

She was so pale, you could
almost see through her.
"It could be . . . ours," she whispered.

"Whose?" asked Nicky, Vicky, Alex, Yasmin, and Po.
"What did she say?" asked Mrs. Dimitros.

"Ours!"
she said louder.

"Well, whoever's it is, it needs to come off the road," said Stella's mom . . .

and when Dad came home that afternoon, he found an old bus where the front yard used to be. "The wheels stick out onto the sidewalk," he said. "There are sure to be regulations. . . ."

"Well, it's staying here," said Stella.
"That's my regulation."

Next morning, Stella looked out her front window.
People were sitting on the wall, where no one had sat before.

Under the bus were Esther, Rajit, Chelsea, and Charles.
"Mommy," said Stella, "I'm going out." And she joined them.

That day, the bus settled in. Weeds nudged up around the tires. Snails made silver trails, and a pair of sparrows nested in the old engine.

While the children played, the grown-ups mopped and scrubbed and polished.

That night, the bus got a bit of new paint.

"Hello, boys!" said Mom. "I've got an idea! Come back tomorrow—
and you can paint the whole bus. Make it sparkle."

Next morning, Stella drew a picture for the Ratz to copy.

People came with donations.

Popi brought her goldfish, Eric.

Luke gave a set of Supercomix.

Stella carried in her table soccer with the missing goalie.

Mrs. Stavros brought a bus cake.

And Lucy lent her dog, Bear—for anyone who needed to just sit and pat something.

Life returned to the old bus.
Stella's fingers fluttered and her soccer players spun.

Babies crawled,

people laughed,

kids fought,

granddads scratched dogs,

meetings were planned,

couples met,

and the Fingles showed their vacation pictures.

One Saturday morning,
just outside Stella's house,
there was music and dancing,
there were picnics and laughter . . .

when a tow truck arrived.

"It's against regulations!" said the driver.
"This bus is causing an obstruction."

"He means it sticks out," Stella's dad
whispered.

# "The bus has to go,"

said the driver.

As the front wheels left the ground,
snails dropped from under the bus
and a twittering came from
the old engine.

"Go where?"

gasped the crowd.

"To the
JUNKYARD,"

came the reply.

The crowd pleaded for their bus, but the junkyard boss
came out to join the driver and shook his head.

  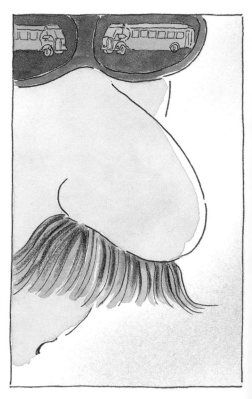

"This one's for the CRUSHER!"

A little pink glow crept across Stella's cheek. Three rescued snails were deep in her pocket. "Excuse me," she said. "Shall we play table soccer?

"You can have the only goalie . . . but if I win, we'll keep the bus."

"And why," asked the junkyard boss, "tell me why
should I play you for the bus?"

"Because," replied Stella, "there are sparrows nesting in the engine."

The game began. Handles spun. The ball smacked end to end, then . . .

# GOAL!

Stella scored.

She followed that with nine more—and won!
The boss put out his hand. "Joe," he said.
"Stella," said Stella. They shook hands.

Then Stella ran to
the front of the bus.

"Come and see," she said. . . .

"Chicks!"

Amid the frantic flapping of the parent sparrows'
wings, Joe the junkyard boss spoke quietly.
"Better get your bus to somewhere safe, kid.
Somewhere out of the way."

"Thank you!" said Stella.

And the crowd cheered.

"I know where we can take it!" said Stella.

While the others pushed, she and Mom sat up front to steer . . .

*almost* back to where they'd started from.

And when the old bus came to rest at last, everyone else needed a rest, too. Well, *almost* everyone.

*As a full moon rose,*
*three snails slid safely back*
*under the tires.*

*And tomorrow, Stella will see*
*the sparrow chicks fly*
*for the first time.*

That evening,
in the vacant lot just behind
Stella's house, music drifted high over the city,
and the grass was danced flat around
a bus called Heaven.